DATE DUE

AUG 11 1994		
JAN 04 1996		
DEC 16 1996		
MAR 02 1999		
FEB 27 2003		
AUG 27 2003		
AUG 07 2005		
JUL 26 2007		
JAN 25 2008		
OCT 26 2011		
AUG 03 2012		
SE 04 '12		
NO 08 '12		
DEC 05 2012		
SE 0 ° 'IF		
JUN 27 2017		

GAYLORD

A JUST ONE MORE BOOK
Just For You

Sillyhen's Big Surprise

by Valerie Tripp

Illustrated by Sandra Kalthoff Martin

Developed by The Hampton-Brown Company, Inc.

 CHILDRENS PRESS ®

CHICAGO

Word List

Give children books they can read by themselves, and they'll always ask for JUST ONE MORE. This book is written with 100 of the most basic words in our language, all repeated in an appealing rhythm and rhyme.

a	even	little	said	wall
again	everywhere	lived	seemed	was
all			she	way
and	feathers	make	shined	week
another	feed	more	shiny	what
are	flapped	move	shout	who
as	for	Mrs.	Sillyhen	will
ask		much	smaller	wise
at	get	must	speak	with
away	glow	my	so	
	grow		stay	you
before		need	stop	
began	had	next		
big(ger)	her	nice	terrible	
but	here's	no	than	
	house	now	that	
came			the	
can	I	of	then	
chicken(s)	if	oh	there('s)	
clean(ed)	in	one	tiny	
come	is(n't)	out	to	
	it('s)		told	
day		pop	too	
dear	just			
decided		remember		
do	kept	right		
door	know	room		
Duck				

Library of Congress Cataloging-in-Publication Data
Tripp, Valerie, 1951-
Sillyhen's big surprise / by Valerie Tripp ; illustrated by Sandra Kalthoff Martin.
p. cm. — (A Just one more book just for you)
Summary: Wishing her little house were larger, Sillyhen follows her wise neighbor's advice to invite more chickens to come and stay.
ISBN 0-516-01522-2
[1. Chickens — Fiction. 2. Stories in rhyme.] I. Martin, Sandra Kalthoff, ill. II. Title. III. Series.
PZ8.3.T698Sq 1989
[E] — dc20
89-35758
CIP
AC

Sillyhen lived in a nice little house.
She kept it clean and shiny.
Then one day she decided
her house was much too tiny.

3

4

Dear Mrs. Duck, what can I do
to make my little house grow?
You are so wise. If there's a way
to do it you will know.

Sillyhen, there is a way.
Now here's what you must do.
Ask a chicken right away
to come and stay with you.

Right away a chicken came
to stay with Sillyhen.

But in a week she had to speak
to the duck next door again.

Oh Mrs. Duck, it's terrible!
No room to move at all!
There's chicken feed just everywhere
and feathers wall to wall!

8

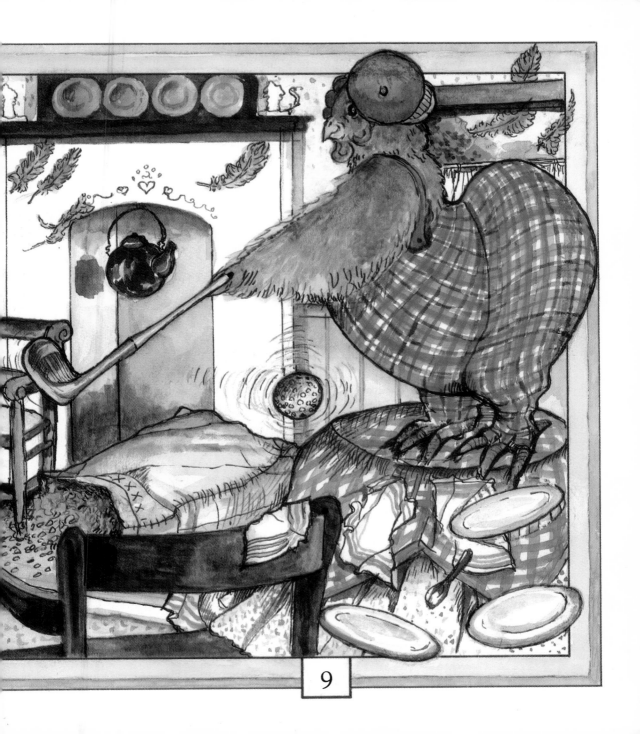

9

Dear Mrs. Duck, what can I do?
I need more room, MUCH more!
For my house isn't bigger now.
It's smaller than before!

Sillyhen there IS a way.
Now here's what you must do.
Ask another chicken
to come and stay with you.

Right away a chicken came
to stay with Sillyhen.

But in a week she had to speak to the duck next door again.

Oh Mrs. Duck, it's terrible!
No room to move at all!
There's chicken feed just everywhere
and feathers wall to wall!

12

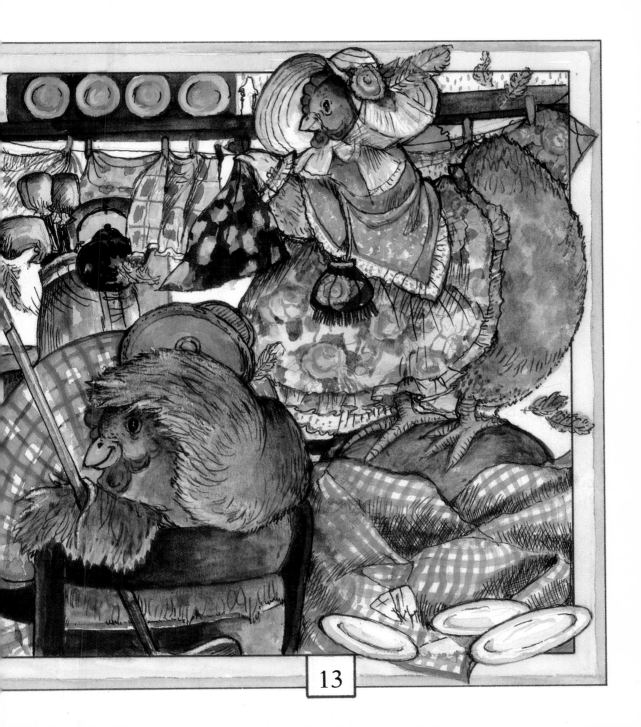

Dear Mrs. Duck, what can I do?
I need more room, much MORE!
My house is even smaller now,
much smaller than before!

Sillyhen there IS a way.
Now here's what you must do.
Ask JUST ONE MORE chicken
to come and stay with you.

But...
One more chicken was too much!
The house began to pop!

16

Chickens, chickens everywhere!
And Sillyhen said...

Sillyhen flapped her feathers,
and she began to shout,

 No more chickens in my house!

Sillyhen cleaned and Sillyhen shined
to make the little house glow,
and as she cleaned it seemed to her
the house began to...

GROW!

With no more chickens in the way,
her house was nice again,
and it seemed very, very big
for just one Sillyhen!

So now you know just what to do
to make a little house grow.
Ask chickens to come stay with you.
Remember who told you so!